RECON ACADEMY

FILE NO. 1457578

MIXED SIGNALS

BY CHRIS EVERHEART
ILLUSTRATED BY ARCANA STUDIO

ACCESS GRANTED ▶▶▶▶

D1424313

Raintree is an imprint of Capstone Global Library Limited, a company incorporated in England and Wales having its registered office at 264 Banbury Road, Oxford, OX2 7DY – Registered company number: 6695582

www.raintree.co.uk
myorders@raintree.co.uk

Edited by Donnie Lemke
Designed by Brann Garvey and Bob Lentz
Original illustrations © Capstone Global Library Limited 2020
Originated by Capstone Global Library Ltd
Printed and bound in India

ISBN 978 1 4747 8433 7
23 22 21 20 19
10 9 8 7 6 5 4 3 2 1

British Library Cataloguing in Publication Data
A full catalogue record for this book is available from the British Library.

›CONTENTS

ENTER

›GADGETRY

›MARTIAL ARTS

›COMPUTERS

›FORENSICS

TEAM BREAKDOWN

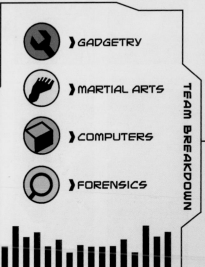

Born into a world of rising threat —

— they witnessed terror strike the safety of their town.

As they grew up, each member developed a unique ability . . .

FEDERAL B

FORENSICS

MARTIAL ARTS

COMPUTERS

GADGETRY

In the corridors of Seaside High, the four of them united.

They combined their skills and formed the most high-tech and secret security force on Earth.

SEASIDE HIGH SCHOOL

RECON ACADEMY

CONTINUE >>>>

SECTION

ACCESS GRANTED 》》》》

JAY
GADGETRY

128718
293829
9283
98289
89
1
109201
192091
1992

9

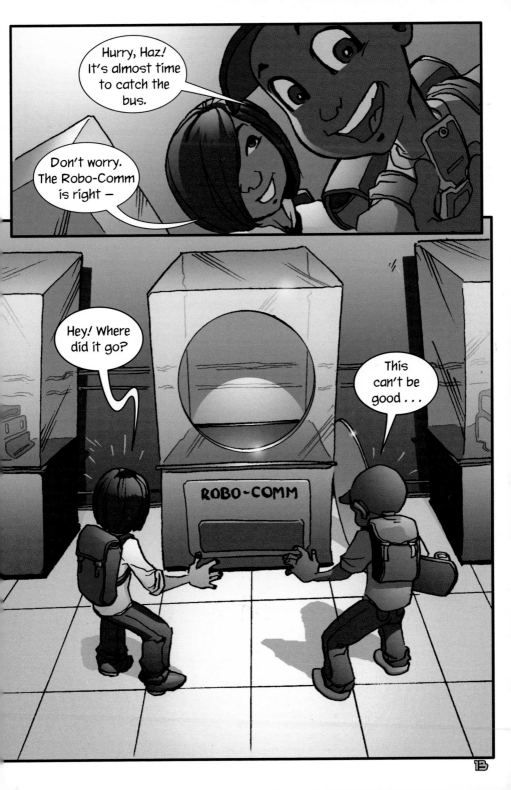

SECTION

2

ACCESS GRANTED ⟩⟩⟩⟩

HAZMAT
FORENSICS

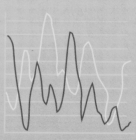

128718
293829
9283
98289
89
1
109201
192091
1992

Look, Jay! tyre tracks!

Come on, Haz! We have to follow them!

They lead inside that door.

There's the guard.

So where's the Robo-Comm?

It's a message from Jay.

Isn't he on a field trip with Hazmat today?

BEEP! BEEP! BEEP!

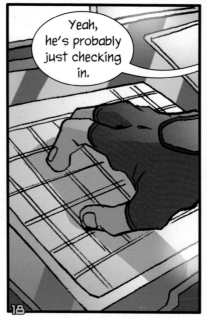

Yeah, he's probably just checking in.

**** AT MUSEUM ****

MISS **** YOU ****

DATE **** LATER

Weird. The message is a bit garbled.

I'm calling in Ryker and Emmi!

SHADOW CELL AT MUSEUM! NEED BACKUP NOW!

"Sale at the museum"? Sweet!

And they're coming back now with our gifts!

S****ELL AT MUSEUM!**** BACK**** NOW****

How long will it take for Emmi and Ryker to get here?

I'm not sure.

But we have to slow down Shadow Cell until they arrive.

I'll access the museum's floor plan and see if there's a rear entrance.

That's weird. I can't get into the museum's system.

SECTION

ACCESS GRANTED >>>>

RYKER
COMPUTERS

128718
293829
9283
98289
89
1
109201
192091
1992

1827178   198291821   919298

1827178   198291821   918298

Meanwhile . . .

Those guys should have come back with their class.

They're going to be in serious trouble.

It's a message from Haz.

AT**E*VENT***
SERVING SP*G*ITY**
S**ELL**ING OUT
FAST****HURRY!

An invitation to a spaghetti dinner?

Now they're just teasing us. They get to have all the fun.

And the spaghetti . . .

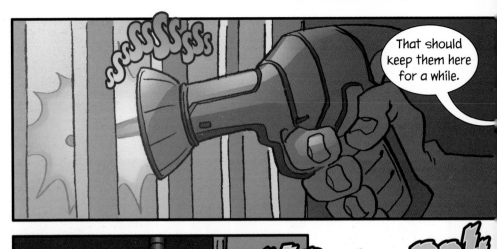

That should keep them here for a while.

KKKKRRRRRRRR!!

OPEN

KLIK!

Oh no! It didn't work!

I don't get it. I had it set right. It should have fried the lock!

Let's get moving.

Load it up.

Jay, I don't think we can wait for Emmi and Ryker.

You're right. They're going to take the Robo-Comm right now!

This is bad.

It gets worse.

Hurry up! Our window of opportunity is closing.

Jay, we're tied up, Shadow Cell is about to take the Robo-Comm, and our backup hasn't arrived yet!

How could things possibly get any worse?!

Well . . . I don't think our backup is coming.

SECTION

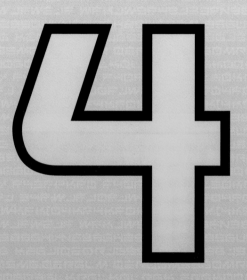

4

ACCESS GRANTED ⟩⟩⟩⟩

EMMI
MARTIAL ARTS

8579
1564574
109201
192091
1992
745979

128718
293829
9283
88289
89
1
109201
192091
1992

Where in the world are Haz and Jay?

Well, an invitation to a spaghetti dinner *is* hard to pass up.

Wait a second!

This isn't an invitation. It's a scrambled message!

Did they code their messages?

No. All of their messages have been jumbled by some kind of interference.

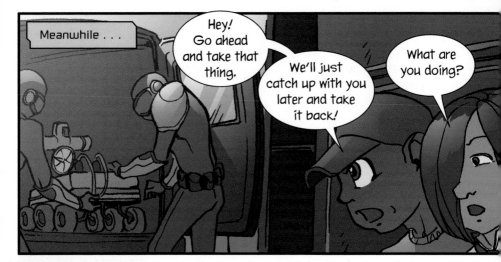

Meanwhile . . .

Hey! Go ahead and take that thing.

We'll just catch up with you later and take it back!

What are you doing?

Grab them. They're coming along.

You should have kept quiet, kid.

Was this part of your plan, Jay?

It's perfect!

THUNK!

43

Meanwhile, outside the museum . . .

Come on!

Where is everybody? There are no guards or anyone watching the place.

Can you get a lock on them?

No, everything's all scrambled.

45

SECTION

ACCESS GRANTED ⟩⟩⟩⟩

RECON ACADEMY
SECRET SECURITY FORCE

128718
293829
9283
98289
89
1
109201
192091
1992

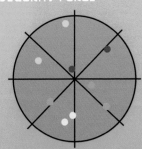

47

We lost them!

I can't get a lock on them, but I have a general direction.

They're still in the city, and —

Huh? That's weird.

What?

I think the van just stopped.

49

Emmi, I'm getting a signal! They're close!

Let's go!

Thanks for your help, kids!

Just doing our jobs!

There's still time. They're only a couple of streets away.

Let's hope Jay and Haz are ready to fight their way out.

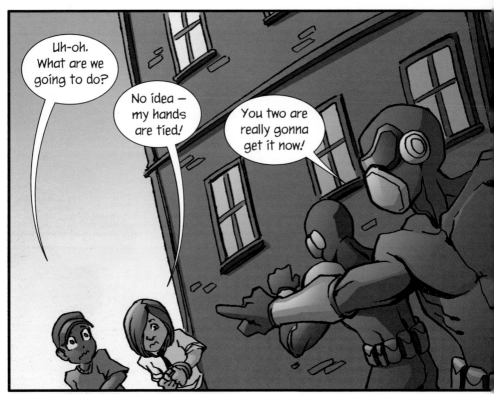

SMAAACK!

THUD!

WHAP!

That'll teach 'em to mess with Recon!

Yeah!

But next time you guys go out for a spaghetti dinner, call me *first*.

What's she talking about, Haz?

I think she just asked you out.

Huh?!

SPYSPACE

a place for international spies

CHAT ROOM PROFILES

NAME: Jeremiah Johnson

AGE: 13

HEIGHT: 1.65 metres

WEIGHT: 54 kilograms

EYES: brown

HAIR: none

SPY ORG: Recon Academy

SPECIAL ABILITIES: Gadget guru and a totally gnarly skateboarder

NAME: Matthew Hazner

AGE: 13

HEIGHT: 1.67 metres

WEIGHT: 57 kilograms

EYES: brown

HAIR: black

SPY ORG: Recon Academy

SPECIAL ABILITIES: Forensics, specializing in fingerprint analysis, ballistics, bloodstain pattern analysis, toxicology

PHOTOS

INSTANT CHAT
recent posts   see all

Hey, Jay! How'd your date with Emmi go?

Very funny, Hazmat. You know that it was all a big misunderstanding.

Yeah, we've sure had a lot of MIXED SIGNALS lately ;) Btw, whatever happened to the communications jammer thingamajig?

You mean, Robo-Comm?

Did the cops find a safe place to store it? I wouldn't want Robo-Comm to fall into the wrong hands again.

Don't worry! I'll keep my eyes on it.

You?! The cops gave you Robo-Comm? Why do you need a communications jammer?

Everyone needs a little privacy, Haz...

Jay? Jay? Are you there?...............

› CASE FILE

CASE: "Mixed Signals"
CASE NUMBER: 9781474784337
AGENTS: Jay and Hazmat
ORGANIZATION: Recon Academy

SUBJECT: Espionage

OVERVIEW: A division of Shadow Cell focuses heavily on espionage to gather intelligence on their targets. Lately, Shadow Cell has attempted to acquire high-tech spy equipment, such as the Robo-Comm communications jammer, from high-security locations nation-wide.

METHODS:
- black bag operations
- surveillance
- cryptography

INTELLIGENCE:

espionage act of spying, or the work of a spy in trying to gain secret information

data theft stealing information or facts through espionage

intelligence information or data

METHODS OF ESPIONAGE:

BLACK BAG OPERATIONS: illegal entry into buildings to gather intelligence or secret data. This process often involves: breaking and entering, lock picking, safe cracking, fingerprinting, photography, surveillance and many other spy skills.

SURVEILLANCE: secretly observing someone or something to get information. Surveillance actually means "to watch over" in French. It can also involve eavesdropping (listening in on private communications) to steal information.

CRYPTOGRAPHY: involves two skills — encryption and decryption. Encryption involves turning messages into unreadable code so that only certain people can read it by deciphering the code. Decryption, on the other hand, is when you crack (solve) a code so that you can read confidential messages that were meant for someone else.

CONCLUSION:

As members of Recon Academy, Hazmat and Jay have been trained to know the difference between spying and stealing. They use careful planning and stay within the law to protect the greater good. But Recon members never hesitate to put a spanner in Shadow Cell's shady plans!

› ABOUT THE AUTHOR

Chris Everheart always dreamed of interesting places, fascinating people and exciting adventures. He is still a dreamer. He enjoys writing thrilling stories about young heroes who live in a world that doesn't always understand them. Chris lives in Minnesota, USA, with his family. He plans to travel to every continent on Earth, see interesting places, meet fascinating people and have exciting adventures.

› ABOUT THE ILLUSTRATOR

Arcana Studios, Inc. was founded by Sean O'Reilly in British Columbia, Canada, in 2004. Arcana has since established itself as Canada's largest comic book and graphic novel publisher. A nomination for a Harvey Award and winning the "Schuster Award for Top Publisher" are just a couple of Arcana's accolades. The studio is known as a quality publisher for independent comic books and graphic novels.

GLOSSARY

access get information from a computer

beacon light or sound used as a signal or warning

decode turn something that is written in code into ordinary language

garbled mixed up and not making sense

interference when something interrupts a signal or message so that you can't see or hear it properly

sensors instruments that can detect changes in heat, sound or pressure

1. Team Recon uses all sorts of cool gadgets. If you could have any device from this story, which one would you want? Why?

2. Which member of Team Recon is your favourite? What do you like about him or her?

3. Each member of Team Recon has a special ability. Jay is great with gadgets, Emmi is a martial arts expert, Ryker is a computer whizz and Hazmat has a knack for detective work. Which member of Team Recon do you think is most important? Why?

1. Jay and Hazmat get in trouble and have to rely on their friends to help them. Have you ever had to count on someone else to get something done? How did it turn out? Write about it.

2. Design your own useful gadget. What does it do? How does it work? What would you use this cool new tool of yours to do? Write about it. Then, draw a picture of your new gadget.

3. Jay's messages to Emmi and Ryker get scrambled and cause confusion for Team Recon. Have you ever sent a message or said something that was misunderstood by someone else? What happened? Write about your miscommunication.